HOPE
STAYS
HOME

Regina Stephenson

Illustrated by Daniel Majan

To order additional copies of this book, contact:
Xlibris
844-714-8691
www.Xlibris.com
Orders@Xlibris.com

ISBN: Softcover   978-1-6641-2893-4
       EBook   978-1-6641-2892-7

Print information available on the last page

Rev. date: 09/04/2020

HOPE STAYS HOME

Dedications

Dedicated to my Queens
Taylor, Kayla, and Layla
Love you immensely

Hope Stays Home

Sunday fun day. Turns my bathtub into a bubble bath slime making museum.

Monday madness.
Turns into an all day
movie marathon.

Tuesday taco night.
Turns my kitchen into
all-you-can-eat taco bar.

Wednesday gets even wackier. When my daddy does my hair in his man cave.

Thursday play dates
become virtual
play dates.

Friday is even more fantastic. When Mom and I face paint in the family room.

Saturday at the Waffle
House. Turns my
bedroom into a breakfast
in bed Saturday.

At the end of the week. We start all over and my house turns back into a house of Hope.

Printed in the United States
By Bookmasters